I0726541

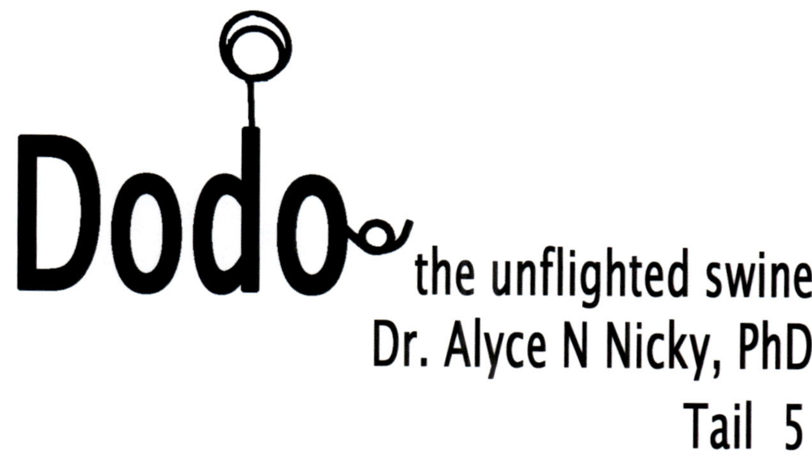

Dodo
the unflighted swine
Dr. Alyce N Nicky, PhD
Tail 5

Tale & Imagery
Terry & Boyd Krueger

WORKBOOK PRESS LLC
187 E Warm Springs Rd,
Suite B285, Las Vegas, NV 89119, USA

Website: https://workbookpress.com/
Hotline: 1-888-818-4856
Email: admin@workbookpress.com

Ordering Information:
Quantity sales. Special discounts are available on quantity purchases by corporations, associations, and others. For details, contact the publisher at the address above.

Library of Congress Control Number:
ISBN-13:   978-1-961845-88-6 (Paperback Version)
             978-1-961845-81-7 (Digital Version)

REV. DATE: 07.17.2023

Friends, real and imagined, mentors of all sorts...
parents, teachers, co-workers and acquaintances,
your words and actions have made an impression.

A special thank you to Juliet,
for her hands in pressing seaweed.

Dodo⸴ woke up and was in a cave of white.

He heard a voice and was suddenly uncovered. It was the woman
who had rescued him. With a friendly "hello," she introduced
herself as Dr. Alyce N Nicky, PhD.

Dr. Nicky informed Dodo⸴ that he had been asleep for three days
and thought he must be very hungry.

Dodo⸴ replied, "I am, I could eat like a pig !"

So, they went to a buffet where they could eat all they wanted.

Eat like a PIG... he did !

The food was so good... but wait a minute...
NO BACON, thank you very much !
Dodo could not believe his good fortune. He was safe and
Dr. Nicky was helping him.

Dodo was really, really full… he said he had really "pigged out,"
but that was OK because he was a pig.

Dr. Nicky and Dodo laughed and settled into conversation.

Dr. Nicky asked Dodo, "What had happened to him such that she had found him all alone in the intertidal ?"

Dodo took a deep breath and started re-telling his story...

He was born in southern California in the San Fernando Valley. He was the last piglet born in a litter of 13. All of his siblings, in fact, everyone in his family had been born with sturdy wings and the ability to fly. Not so of him. He was born with a strange appendage protruding straight up from his back, a weird wing with an odd twist at the tip.

The family Swine had shunned Dodo; so he went off in search of learning to fly...

He had met a girl named Callee who had taught him to swim...

He had thought that there were flying bison in Montana.

He tried to find his way to Montana but ended up being dropped off
at Montaña de Oro state beach, which is in California
not in the state of Montana.

And, while he had wandered the beach,
he was washed into the ocean.

After more days than he could count, he was
washed up on the shore, where he found and followed footprints.
They led nowhere.

Then, while he was resting, he had enjoyed the most wonderful dream
of meeting a pig, just like him and her name was Pearl E Pig.

She had been on a quest for wings, too.
And, she had found hers at a butterfly sanctuary...

and she was beautiful !

Then, after waking from his dream and feeling forlorned,
he stared out into the intertidal and saw her.
He was not certain if she was real, or just his imagination.

He proceeded to tell her about all of the creatures
he had encountered while afloat in the ocean. Really,
they were all just different pieces of seaweed floating along.

At that point, Dr. Nicky stated "that is exactly the research that I do" !
Dodo looked at her and asked if she would explain.

Dr. Nicky explained that she had earned her doctoral degree (a PhD)
in Phycology which is the study of seaweed.

Dr. Nicky told Dodo about her adventure of completing a course
of study which had taken her all over the world.

She would sample different seaweed in the intertidal,
mudflats, or open water, then
transport it back to her laboratory and begin her research.

Dodo⸎ listened in awe to her story. He, too, had developed
a great fondness for seaweed as it had kept him alive
until he reached shore again.

Dr. Nicky and Dodo᷍ talked for hours.

he was exhausted after his first day back in the real world.

Dr. Nicky suggested that they call it a day and go home

Dodo᷍ agreed and off they went.

As they talked, and drove towards home, Dr. Nicky told Dodo˞ that seaweed come in many different varieties and colors, and they can be beautiful.

She told Dodo˞ that whenever she samples seaweed, she always collects enough samples to be included in her herbarium.

Dodo˞ asked what an herbarium was. After Dr. Nicky parked, they went to the rear of her car and showed him one of her seaweed presses.

They went into her lab.
"It is quite a lot of fun" she enthusiastically exclaimed.
"Let me show you some photos."

First you select a particular piece of seaweed. Next, arrange it
on the herbarium paper and cover it. Then, you place newsprint
between the pressing sheets to absorb water.
Finally, all is layered together and tightened.

After a period of time, the seaweed dries.
When the press is opened, the result is seaweed art.

Dr. Nicky told Dodo⌁ that she places these dried seaweed sheets
in her herbarium which becomes like an seaweed museum.
Then if she ever needs samples for research,
she can always select the ones she needs.

Dodo⌁ just sat there staring at her.

Dr. Nicky asked, " What's wrong ?"

Dodo⌁ replied, "All he had ever thought about was learning to fly.
But there is so much more in this world.

What a day !

And it wasn't over, Dr. Nicky treated Dodo to
roasted marshmallows

She showed him how to hold the marshmallow over the fire
so it would get roasted just right, and then
how to eat it right off of the stick.

Deeeeelicious !

After they were satisfied with sweetness, Dr. Nicky said that she
was chairing a conference (lots of people talking about science)
the following day.

But she said she had a friend who maintined a butterfly sanctuary
and that she had arranged for Dodo to spend the day with her
so he could learn all about Monarch butterflies.

Dr. Nicky thought that Dodo would enjoy the visit
since in his dream of Pearl E Pig, she had butterfly wings.

Dodo was really excited because after all, wings were still
on the bucket list for this little pig with a strange appendage
protruding straight up from his back, a weird wing
with an odd twist at the tip.

Off they both went to bed.

The following day, Dr. Nicky dropped Dodo off at the
Monarchsery, a Monarch Waystation.

She told him that she would be back to pick him up later.

"Enjoy your day and the Monarch butterflies," she said.

As Dodo walked through the waystation entrance,
it was like a forest of milkweed.

He was very excited about his day.

9 781961 845886